★ ★ ★ ★

TONY JEFFERSON IN

Burning Question

Agnes M. Hagen

New Readers Press

For my loyal fan club.

Burning Question
ISBN 1-56420-279-8
Copyright © 2001
New Readers Press
U.S. Publishing Division of Laubach Literacy
1320 Jamesville Avenue, Syracuse, New York 13210

Printed in the United States of America
9 8 7 6 5 4 3 2 1

Director of Acquisitions and Development: Christina Jagger
Content Editor: Terrie Lipke
Copy Editor: Nancy Izuno
Production Director: Heather Witt
Designer: Kimbrly Koennecke
Cover Designer: Kimbrly Koennecke
Cover Illustrator: James P. Wallace
Production Specialist: Alexander Jones

All proceeds from the sale of New Readers Press materials support literacy programs in the United States and worldwide.

Chapter 1

At first, I thought it was my alarm clock that woke me. But after a few seconds, I recognized the sound of howling sirens. I jumped out of bed and ran to the window. Fire! Red and orange flames reflected off the ice-covered trees.

I threw on some clothes and headed down the stairs to my office. My German shepherd, Chance, beat me to the door. The weather report had predicted freezing rain. What an awful night for a fire. I pulled on my warmest coat and boots before chasing Chance out to the slick sidewalk. The icy rain stung my face as I slowly plodded up New Street toward the fire.

As I got closer, I could see flames shooting out of the windows of the Turner Building. The building housed the Turner Furniture Store on the lower floors. The mayor and other local officials had offices on the upper floors.

Chance and I shivered in the cold air. We watched firefighters struggle to put out the flames. Water formed puddles at their feet and turned to ice. Police officer Harry Lyman, a good friend of mine, skidded up to me.

"Hey, Tony, what a night!" he roared. "This weather has been hard on the fire department. They've managed to keep the fire from spreading, but the Turner Building looks like a total loss."

"What a pity," I replied. I'd heard that Bob Turner had been having a hard time lately. "Turner's business has really suffered since that discount place opened up near the mall."

"Yeah," Harry said. "I just hope he wasn't desperate enough—"

"You don't think Bob Turner is responsible for the fire, do you?" I asked with surprise. "Everyone knows how dedicated Bob is. He and his wife, Janet, sacrificed for years to get that business going."

"It's hard to say what a man might do in that situation," Harry replied with a shrug. "The fire chief says it could be arson since the building burned so fast."

I scanned the townspeople who had gathered at the scene. "I don't see Mayor Cook," I said.

"He's out of town," Harry replied. "We paged him, but he hasn't called in yet."

Harry and I watched silently as clouds of thick black smoke billowed from the charred building. It would be hours before it was safe for arson investigators to search for the source of the fire. Bob Turner stood motionless on the sidewalk with his arm around his sobbing wife.

By the time Chance and I walked home, the sun was up. I thawed out in a hot shower while coffee brewed. Then I ate breakfast. I couldn't get the fire out of my mind.

Everyone in Stanton knew the story of the Turner Building. It was a local landmark. Bob Turner had built the huge five-story building for his store and warehouse. In the 1970s, Turner Furniture was the biggest business in Stanton. Folks came from all around to shop there.

But by 1985, sales were slower and Bob had cut back to using only the first two floors. At that time, the mayor was looking for a place to build new offices. The Turner Building was right in the center of town, a perfect location. Now, just a burned-out shell of a building sat in its place.

The fire reminded me of when I was a cop in Baltimore. Fires, burglaries, and murders occurred there every day. I'll never forget the day my partner was gunned down right in front of me. I couldn't save him. For the first time in my life, I didn't want to be a cop. So I left my career behind and moved to rural Virginia.

My grandparents welcomed me into their home in Bath County. And I quickly made new friends. It has been more than a year since I opened this private detective office in Stanton.

Chance and I live in a small apartment above my office. He was a member of the Baltimore police force, too, before an injury sidelined him. And now, he's my partner. That nose of his has helped me find some missing people. And it has even saved my life once or twice.

Chapter 2

My friend Julie stopped by later in the morning. She lives out near my grandparents. We met when I first moved down here. Julie works in Stanton, so we get together often.

"I heard about the fire," Julie said. "It's all over the news. I went to see the Turner Building, but I still can't believe it!"

"Me, neither," I said. "And I was up half the night watching it burn."

"My friend on the city council told

me they're still trying to locate the mayor," Julie said, leaning against my desk. "He's supposed to be in South Carolina, but no one's been able to reach him."

"He can't be around here, or the fire sirens would have gotten him out of bed, too," I replied with a chuckle.

Just then, Harry came in the door. "How're you doing, Tony?" he asked in a raspy voice. "I hope you got more sleep than I did last night."

"Nah, I was too wound up to go back to bed," I told him. "I hear you still haven't spoken to Mayor Cook."

"Nope," Harry said, helping himself to a cup of coffee. "We talked to a buddy of his in South Carolina. The mayor was supposed to fly in last night for a few days of golfing. But we called the airline, and he never got on the plane."

"Where could he be?" Julie asked. "He has lived alone since his wife died.

I think his only relative is his sister in New Jersey."

"Have you checked with his secretary?" I asked. "He may have changed his travel plans."

"We sent an officer to talk to her," Harry answered. "Those two have worked together for a long time. She must know where he is."

"How did the fire start?" Julie asked.

"There's no official word on that yet," Harry said. "But a team of arson investigators is working on it right now. The building is in bad shape, so they have to be careful. It might take a while to find the kind of evidence they're looking for."

"Evidence of a crime?" I asked with my usual curiosity.

Before Harry could answer, we were interrupted by the ring of his cell phone. "Lyman here . . . oh, no . . . I've got to run, Tony," Harry gasped. "That was the fire chief. They found a body in the Turner Building."

Harry ran out, and the door slammed shut behind him. Julie got up to leave, too.

"I can't believe it," she said. "It was bad enough to lose the building."

"Yeah, I know," I agreed. "Now I'm even more curious about how the fire started."

Julie headed out the door. "I've got to get back to work, Tony," she said. "Call me if you hear anything else."

Chapter 3

The day turned out to be full of sadness and surprises. In the afternoon, I got a lead on a teenaged runaway I'd been trying to track down. After several phone calls, I located the girl down in St. Louis. She was living with a friend she met on the Internet. Her parents were relieved to hear that she was OK. But it was hard for me to tell them that their 17-year-old daughter was not coming home.

After supper, I checked in with

Harry. He told me the fire department had confirmed that a man's body was found in the Turner Building. The coroner from Roanoke had been called in to assist with the autopsy. Still, it might take some time to identify the body. But I had a feeling I already knew who the victim was.

I stretched out in my easy chair to read the newspaper. I was planning to go to bed early. Then I heard Chance barking. I went down the stairs to my office and found him pawing at the front door. A woman was peering through the frost-covered window.

I shooed Chance out of the way and opened the door. The woman turned to look behind her and then quickly slipped into my office. Even in the dim light of the entryway, I recognized her.

"Mrs. Turner?" I asked.

"Janet, please," she replied.

I took her coat and led her to a chair. "And I'm Tony Jefferson," I said. "It's nasty out there tonight. Would you like something hot to drink?"

Janet nodded.

"What will it be—coffee, tea, or hot cocoa?" I offered.

"Tea, please," she said quietly. "Don't go to any trouble."

"It's no trouble at all," I told her. "I was just going to have some myself." I put the water on to boil. "How about a cookie?" I opened a tin of my grandmother's molasses cookies and set them on my desk.

"I didn't know who else to turn to," she said. "Please, you mustn't tell my husband that I came here. But I need your help." Janet Turner sounded desperate. She was near tears.

I nodded. "You shouldn't worry about that," I tried to reassure her. "In this business, I'm trusted with all kinds of secrets. If people don't tell me, I find them out anyway. It's my job."

Janet seemed nervous and fragile.

She was a birdlike woman with sharp blue eyes. I handed her a cup of tea. Her long thin fingers trembled as she grasped it.

"Mr. Jefferson," she began, "I can't believe I'm saying this. I think my daughter-in-law set our store on fire." She sighed heavily. "The police have been asking questions, and I don't know what to tell them." Clearly, she didn't get any more sleep than I did. Tears welled up in her tired eyes.

"I think the police and fire departments are just trying to get all the information they can," I told her. "As far as I know, they still believe the fire could be an accident."

I didn't really buy that, but I thought it might help calm her down. Harry told me he'd talked to Bob Turner. But I didn't realize the police had questioned his wife. As long as she trusted me, I would try to find out what she knew about the fire.

Chapter 4

"The police suspect my husband, Bob," Janet Turner sighed. "I've known him for almost 40 years. He'd never do something like that!" She lowered her head and dabbed at her eyes with a tissue. "I thought maybe you could help me prove his innocence."

"Well, I can't interfere with the ongoing investigation," I explained. "But maybe I can help in some way. What makes you suspect your daughter-in-law was involved?"

Janet's voice was barely a whisper. And even though we were alone, she kept looking around nervously as if she was afraid that someone might overhear.

"I just found out that my son, Dirk, has been asking Bob for a loan," Janet said. "Dirk's had a hard time lately. His job doesn't really pay much. And it seems that Nancy's not happy no matter what he does. I know she's pressuring him to get money from us."

"Maybe the police have already spoken to Dirk and Nancy," I said. "Where do they live?"

"They live a couple of hours from here," she replied. "They're driving down tomorrow. Bob talked to Dirk. He said Dirk was still pressing him for money. But if we loan him money now, we'll never be able to retire."

"So you and Bob were planning to retire soon?" I asked.

"Bob is so tired all the time," she

said. "I don't know how much longer he can work. Last month, we visited this wonderful retirement village. There's a lake and a golf course. We fell in love with the place. But it's expensive. We would have to sell the store for a good price. That could take a while."

Janet paused for a sip of tea. It was late in the evening, and everything downtown was closed. But she still periodically glanced at the door, like she was afraid of being seen.

"What if Nancy couldn't wait?" she asked. "Dirk used to work for us. She knows Bob has good insurance."

"Janet," I said, "I think you're worrying too much. Let's see what the investigation turns up. In the meantime, I'll try to find out if Nancy was in town yesterday. If she wasn't, then you have nothing to worry about. I know that you're upset. Losing the furniture store must be a terrible shock to you and your husband. Go home and try to relax. There's nothing more you can do right now."

"Thank you, Mr. Jefferson," she said. "It helps to have someone to talk to. I don't want to burden my husband with any of this."

It was after 9 P.M. when she finally left. I sat in my office, looking out the window. The sleet had turned to rain.

Janet's visit left me with more questions than answers. Did Nancy really have a motive to drive here and set the fire? What about Dirk? If he was desperate for money, maybe he was involved. Bob Turner needed the money too. But would he burn down his own store?

Chapter 5

The next morning, Harry came in, stamping his feet and complaining about the cold weather. "Is the coffee on, Tony?" he wheezed.

"This weather's getting to you," I said.

"Yeah, and it looks like I'm going to be working overtime, too," he groaned as he sat down.

"How come?" I asked, pushing a cup of coffee toward him.

"Well, we got the report," he said.

"The Turner Building fire was arson. They've identified four or five places where the fire was set."

"I was afraid of that," I said, shaking my head slowly.

"That's not all," Harry said. "We got the coroner's report on that body the firefighters found. The report says the man was murdered before the fire got to him. Worse yet, the victim was Mayor Cook."

I nodded. "I had a feeling that was why no one could find him," I said.

"Look, Tony," Harry said, "we need all the help we can get on this. Would you do a little research for me? I need anything you can find on Mayor Cook, Bob Turner, and a guy named Jim Williams." Harry gulped some coffee and stood up to leave.

"Sure, Harry, but before you go, who's Jim Williams?" I asked.

"Jim Williams is the closest thing Bob Turner had to an enemy," Harry replied. "He's a big-shot real estate developer. He came to town about a year and a half ago with the idea of making a fortune developing some of our land. He and Bob knocked heads at some city-council meetings.

"Jim had plans for downtown Stanton. He wanted to build a new theater, art museum, and that kind of stuff. Of course, he planned to get rid of the old stores, like Turner Furniture."

I nodded to Harry as he said good-bye and hurried out the door. Now that he mentioned it, I remembered reading in the newspaper about some lively city-council meetings. At the time, it didn't seem important. Now, I suspected there was more to the story.

That afternoon, I went right to my computer to look up information for Harry. Stanton's mayor had a clean record. It was hard to find anyone who had something bad to say about him. Bob Turner was just as well liked. He had done good things for this town. He sponsored festivals and fund drives. And he was proud to have the mayor's office above his store.

When I started looking into Jim Williams, things got interesting. Williams liked to find centrally located Southern towns and turn them into cash cows. First, he'd build cultural centers, restaurants, and shops. Then, he'd put up apartments and sit back and watch the money come in. If one town didn't work out, he'd just move on to the next one. I wondered if Stanton would be one of his successes—

Just then, Julie burst into my office, interrupting my train of thought. "Are you still working?" she called to me. "It's almost seven. Have you eaten?"

"It's that late?" I asked her.

"It's barbecue night at the Robin's Nest," Julie said. "Let's go unwind."

"That's a great idea," I decided. "Just let me close up."

Chapter 6

I'd forgotten how much fun barbecue night at the Robin's Nest could be. A country-music band had people dancing and singing along. Platters of barbecued ribs and chicken were served family style.

Julie and I stuffed ourselves full of good food. We talked about the mayor and the Turner Building. I told Julie that word about the mayor's death would be out in time for the ten o'clock news.

"So if the fire didn't kill Mayor Cook, what did?" Julie asked.

"I'm not sure yet," I said. "Harry didn't go into details."

The music stopped as the band left the stage for a break. The room was fairly quiet when a tall dark-haired man entered the restaurant. I wouldn't have noticed him if Julie hadn't kicked me under the table.

"Who's that?" she whispered.

Looking up, I watched the newcomer as he walked to the back of the room and sat down at a small table. His piercing eyes scanned the crowd. The waitress brought him a glass of water, and the stranger suddenly leaped to his feet. He walked across the dining room toward a man who looked familiar to me. The man was Jim Williams. I had seen a photo of him in one of the articles I found online.

The stranger's booming voice drowned out quiet conversations of nearby diners. He accused Jim Williams of harassment and threatened to run him out of town.

"I know you're the one who set fire to my father's store!" the man screamed. "Why can't you just leave him alone?"

"How dare you accuse me of setting that fire!" Williams countered as he stood up. "Everyone knows your father torched his own place because he was losing money."

As customers stared, the stranger grabbed Williams by the collar, and a fight began. Plates crashed to the floor when a table was knocked over. Both men were swearing and swinging at each other. In minutes, the bartender and bouncer appeared, tearing the two men apart. Williams and the stranger were tossed outside.

At the urging of the owner, the band started playing again. The place was cleaned up quickly. Waiters and

Burning Question

waitresses rushed out with platters of food and hollered for folks to dig in.

"Was that Dirk Turner?" I asked a waitress as she refilled our drinks.

"You bet," she replied with a disgusted look. "I'm glad he's not here more often. Only thing he knows how to do is cause trouble."

After dinner, Julie said she was tired. So I told her I was, too, and we both went home. In truth, I couldn't wait to get back to my computer.

I decided to check out Nancy and Dirk Turner. This search was more fruitful than I'd expected. Dirk had done time twice for assault and battery. And, Nancy, was the mayor's niece. That seemed like an odd coincidence. Nancy's record was clean, though. There was nothing about her that would make her an arson suspect.

I worked pretty late, but I managed to get a few hours of sleep before the phone woke me. It was Harry.

"What a night," he complained. "This weather's causing a lot of accidents. Hey, did you get a chance to do any research for me?"

"Yeah, I was on the Internet all night," I replied. "That Jim Williams is a pretty interesting character. He seems to be just out for a buck, though. I'm not sure he's the type to kill someone or set fires."

"The problem is that we haven't got any leads," Harry said. "So we need to check out everyone."

"What do you know about Dirk Turner?" I asked Harry.

"He's a troublemaker," Harry said. "But he's not around here much anymore. He and his wife live up near Fairmont now. Believe me, if he were still in town, I'd have had him in for questioning already."

Chance was whining to go out, so I dressed quickly and went downstairs. Chance and I walked over to the park.

I picked up a newspaper on the way back. Last night's brawl was on the front page. So I was not surprised when Janet Turner dropped by my office later that morning.

"Please don't let what happened last night turn you against Dirk," she begged. "It's just that he's so upset about the fire. And sometimes Dirk has a problem controlling his temper." Janet seemed just as nervous as the last time we spoke. I had the feeling she wasn't telling me everything.

"Is there anything else I should know?" I asked. "If you want me to help you, you've got to trust me."

"There is, maybe, one thing," Janet gulped. "I discovered it by accident about a week ago. I think my husband is being threatened."

"What makes you think that?" I asked with genuine surprise.

"The other day, I was checking our e-mail, and I saw a letter to Bob from someone I didn't know. I was curious, so I opened it. I think someone wants him dead."

Janet Turner reached into her purse and pulled out a folded piece of paper. She opened it and handed it to me. It was a printout of the e-mail. Beneath a fuzzy photo of a gravestone were the words "Retire or regret it."

"I'll try to find out who sent this," I said. "Have you noticed any changes in Bob's behavior lately?"

"No," she replied. "He spends most of his time at the store."

"And you don't have any idea what this might be about?" I probed.

"No," she replied, "and it scares me."

Chapter 7

One good thing about having a dog is I always have an excuse to go for a walk. So after Janet's visit, I grabbed Chance's leash, and he ran to the door. Maybe the fresh air would help me sort things out.

Chance and I strolled up New Street toward the Turner Building. Yellow tape and warning signs surrounded the scene of the fire. Because support beams were damaged, the fire department was worried about the floors caving in. As I got closer, the fire chief appeared out front.

"Morning, Chief," I called to him.

"Hi, Tony," he replied. "I see Chance dragged you out of your office!"

"I'd never get away from my desk if it weren't for this dog," I said. "Why are you still hanging around here? Isn't the investigation over?"

"We still have some unanswered questions," he said. "We know this fire was set on purpose, but we're not sure how."

"Maybe Chance can help you out," I offered. "He was trained as an arson detection dog. He never got the chance to work at a fire scene, though. Would you mind if he sniffed around a little?"

"I'd appreciate the help," the chief said. "Follow me. I'll show you where the fire started."

Chance used to take his police work very seriously. And he seemed to sense that this was an important job, too. I held his leash loosely while he followed the chief into the ground floor of the blackened building.

"Here's a spot we're pretty sure is a point of origin," the chief reported.

Chance sniffed at the charred remains of what used to be a chair. Then he looked up at me and let out a little bark.

"He may be on to something," I said. "Is it safe to let him snoop around?"

"Yeah, the first floor's pretty solid," he said. "Let's see where he goes."

Chance walked slowly through the rubble, nose to the ground. He headed toward the back door.

"This looks like a pretty small room," I said. "What was in here?"

"I think it was a cleaning-supply closet," the chief said.

Chance was barking now and digging with his paws. Beneath part of a collapsed wall, I saw something shiny. Chance dug around it and uncovered a small can, like a paint can. The label had been burnt off.

"I'll bet Turner kept some varnish and stains in here for touching up furniture," said the chief. "That would explain why our mechanical sniffer didn't detect anything unusual. The same stuff is all over in here, on all the furniture."

"And what a smart way to start a fire—with something that was already here," I said. "But who would have known about this little closet?"

I could tell by the way the chief looked at me that we were thinking the same thing. He called his investigators back to collect the can Chance found.

"If you want to leave the dog here, we can wash that soot off him," offered the chief.

I laughed. Chance loved to get dirty. "Thanks, anyway," I replied. "We'll get cleaned up at home."

Chapter 8

I started back down New Street. I was just passing the courthouse when I remembered that Harry said the deputy mayor set up a temporary office there. I tied Chance's leash to a lamppost and went inside.

The mayor's secretary, Myra Hastings was sorting through boxes of files. She was an older woman who had worked in city hall for more than 30 years. Her eyes peered at me from over her reading glasses.

"You're that investigator, aren't you?" she asked.

"Yes," I responded, "I'm Tony Jefferson. And you must be Mrs. Hastings."

"*Miss* Hastings," she said sternly.

"This must be a difficult time for you," I said. "How are you doing?"

"I'm so busy that there's no time to think about the mayor, really," she said matter-of-factly. "As I told the police, he didn't discuss his personal affairs with me. I didn't even know he was going away until the plane ticket was delivered to the office."

"Gee, I thought you two were close. You worked side by side for so long," I said.

"We had a professional relationship," Myra replied flatly. She pulled out a file, and without looking up, she changed the subject. "You know we're planning a big memorial service for Mayor Cook tomorrow. The whole town will be there."

"Yes," I said, "he was well liked. Would you mind telling me when you saw him last?"

"Mayor Cook was working late that night," she said. "There was a city-council meeting coming up right after his vacation. He told me he was staying a little late to make certain that everything was in order. Then he was going to take a cab to the airport."

"So he was still here when you left that night?" I asked her.

"I'm certain that he was," she told me. "I said good-bye to him on my way out. As I recall, he didn't answer." She cleared her throat. "Now, I have to get these memorial cards to the church."

"I'll walk you out," I said.

Myra's lack of emotion made me think she was holding something back.

We walked out the front door. I grabbed Chance's leash and untied it.

He growled and sniffed at Myra's purse. She took a step back.

"He's not dangerous, is he?" she asked in a huff.

"Not unless you're a criminal," I explained. "He's a trained police dog."

Chance strained to get closer to Myra's purse. He even let out a couple of barks. I pulled him back.

"I'm sorry, Miss Hastings," I said. "I don't know what's gotten into him."

Myra Hastings snorted, "Humph." Then she headed toward the church.

I had to practically drag Chance in the other direction. I couldn't imagine what it was about Myra's purse that had gotten him so excited.

When we got back to the office, I washed the soot off Chance's feet. He lay down for a nap. Then I spent the afternoon gathering more information for Harry. Sometimes, I was tempted to just let him hire me at the police station. I had to keep reminding myself that I didn't want to be a cop anymore.

I had planned to talk with Jim Williams, so I was pleased to find him eating alone that evening in Stanton's cozy Beverly Restaurant. I had heard that Jim spent a lot of time there.

The small dining room was crowded with professional men and women, continuing to work over dinner and drinks. Jim didn't seem bothered when I asked if I might share his table.

"Help yourself," he offered, pushing a menu toward me. "The service is a little slow today, but the food is good."

I introduced myself and sat down. We made small talk about the weather and the parking problems downtown. By the time the waitress brought my chicken-fried steak and biscuits, it was time to change the topic.

"Isn't it terrible what happened to Mayor Cook?" I asked. "This town won't be the same without the Turner Building."

"It's sad that the mayor died like that," Jim admitted. "He was a good man. But Stanton didn't need that dinosaur of a store. We could build something worthwhile in its place—like a theater complex."

Jim had a one-track mind. I tried to steer him back to the topic at hand.

"I heard the fire was set on purpose," I hinted. "I wonder who would do such a thing."

Jim looked at me with distrust. "What did you say your name was?" he asked.

"It's Tony Jefferson," I told him again. "I'm a private detective."

Jim tried to act as if this made no difference to him. But he was suddenly in a hurry to leave.

"Nice meeting you, Mr. Jefferson," he said as he got up. "Maybe we'll run into each other again." I thought I detected a note of insincerity.

Chapter 9

The weather cleared up just in time for the mayor's memorial service. Local businesses closed for the day so that everyone could attend. Stanton's citizens packed the church pews. Bob Turner sat right up front, next to his wife. Janet was dressed in black from head to toe. Nancy and Dirk sat beside them. Right next to Nancy was Mayor Cook's sister. She looked a lot like her brother. Everyone stared straight ahead as the choir sang and the pastor read from the Bible. Several of the mayor's friends, including Bob Turner, spoke emotionally about their grief.

Julie came with me to the service. I pointed out to her a few of the suspects.

Jim Williams, wearing a flashy designer suit, stood in the back of the church with his arms folded across his chest. Julie said he looked bored and out of place.

Myra Hastings was in the third row. We could tell she had been doing a lot of crying. Her eyes were puffy and red. Through most of the service, she hung her head and covered her face with a lacy handkerchief. It surprised me to see her so emotional.

"Keep your eyes and ears open," I whispered to Julie. "I'll bet that the killer is somewhere in this crowd."

When the service ended, everyone slowly rose and filed out of the church. The mood was very somber. Some people paused in the lobby to chat and to console each other. It was cool but sunny, so a few folks even gathered outside.

We walked past the Turners, who were talking to the mayor's sister. Nancy's long hair hid much of her face as she clung to Dirk. Janet Turner was still crying. Bob just stared off into the distance as if he didn't know what to do next.

We followed the crowd outside. Jim Williams stood alone on the sidewalk, smoking.

"I heard the Turners inviting Miss Cook and some others over to their house," Julie told me. "Let's see if we can get an invitation."

"How are you going to do that?" I asked.

"It'll be easy," she replied. "Just watch me."

I worried about Janet's delicate state of mind, and I almost stopped Julie.

But before I could say anything, Julie was at the church door. She spoke to the Turners as they exited the building. I watched her hug Janet and Miss Cook. Then Julie headed back to where I was standing.

"There, that wasn't tough at all," she said with satisfaction. "I can't wait to see Dirk again. He was so worked up when we saw him at the restaurant. And today he looks very distracted. There's definitely something on his mind."

Half an hour later, Julie and I were searching for a place to park on the Turners' crowded street. We finally pulled over to the side of the road and walked two blocks back to the house. As we walked up the driveway, we caught a glimpse of Dirk behind the house chopping firewood. Maybe he was trying to work off some of that aggression we had witnessed at the Robin's Nest.

Bob greeted us at the door. He led us into a large, elegantly furnished living room. Janet was nowhere in sight, but Nancy waved from the kitchen as we walked by. Miss Cook was sitting at the counter, sipping coffee. The dining room was full of people from the memorial service. They chatted quietly and picked at the snacks laid out on the table.

Julie excused herself to go talk to Nancy. Bob was still acting like he was in a fog. I tried to strike up a conversation.

"It must be tough for you, Bob," I said, "to lose both your business and your friend."

"It all seems so unreal," he replied. "My wife's been a nervous wreck since the fire."

"I know that no one has been charged with arson," I said quietly. "But there have been rumors."

"I've heard," Bob spoke calmly. But

while we talked, his hands were clenched around the arms of his chair.

A loud thud startled us both. It was followed by a shrill scream. Bob and I ran to the kitchen. When we got there, Dirk was holding Janet by her neck up against the wall. Janet was trembling with fear.

"What have you been saying about me?" Dirk shouted. "Some cop told me at the church that they want to interview *me* now. I wasn't even here the night of the fire! Do you want to send me back to prison?"

"Leave her alone!" Bob yelled as he grabbed his son and pushed him out the back door.

Janet sank into a kitchen chair and wept softly as Nancy tried to calm her.

"Are you OK?" Julie asked.

"Sure. He . . . he doesn't mean anything by it," Janet sobbed. "It's that temper of his . . . he never could control it. He's always had problems."

"I think we'd better leave," Julie said quietly. "I'll get our coats."

Burning Question

Chapter 10

"Dirk is even more trouble than I thought!" Julie gasped when we were safely outside. "Nancy told me that Bob fired him from the furniture store two years ago. That's when he and Nancy moved. Dirk has had trouble keeping a job. And they're in debt. She says Nancy will probably get some money from the mayor's will, but he wasn't rich. After that, if Bob and Janet don't help them, they'll be broke."

"Why did Bob fire him?" I asked.

"Well, you've seen how he is," Julie said. "Customers were afraid to deal with him. And I get the feeling that Nancy doesn't really trust him, either."

"So he had more than one motive to burn down his father's store," I said, thinking aloud.

"But he wasn't here when the fire started," said Julie.

"How do we know that?" I asked. "The police are going to question him anyway. Maybe I'll talk to Harry about him."

I heard a noise and turned around. Bob Turner was running down the sidewalk to catch up with us.

"Tony!" he cried. "I need to talk to you! I know who set the fire."

Bob was out of breath and panting. He stumbled against a neighbor's fence and grabbed his chest with his right hand. He slumped to his knees, dropping as if in slow motion. I ran to catch him, and he fell into my arms. Julie called 911 on her cell phone while she ran back to the house for help.

Bob gasped for air. He looked at me, and I thought I heard him say, "She . . . she . . ." The ambulance arrived in minutes. Janet and Dirk rode to the hospital with him. Nancy offered to stay with their guests.

Shortly after the ambulance left, Julie and I finally made it to the car.

"What a day!" I said.

"Poor Bob!" Julie cried. "His store burns down, his friend dies, and now this. I hope he'll be OK."

"Me, too," I replied.

Julie went straight home, so I went back to my office alone. There was a message from Harry on my machine. I wanted to talk to him about Dirk, so I called him right away.

"Hey, Harry," I said, "what's up?"

"I heard the call go out on the scanner," Harry said. "I guess you had some excitement at the Turner house."

"Bob had a heart attack," I said. "I'll

call later and check on him."

"What were you guys doing outside?" he asked.

"Julie and I were leaving, and Bob was running after us," I answered. "He said he knew who set the fire."

"Did he tell you?" Harry asked.

"No," I said. "All he could say was 'she.' I have to ask you something, Harry. Dirk said he's being called in for questioning. Do you have reason to suspect him?"

"Not really," Harry said. "We were just hoping to scare him into telling us whatever he knows."

"Oh," I said, "then he has an alibi?"

"He says he worked late and then went out drinking with a friend," Harry replied.

"You don't mind if I check into that, do you?" I asked.

"Are you kidding?" Harry laughed. "Just let me know when you're ready to go on the payroll!"

Chapter 11

I was frustrated. I hadn't learned much that day. Harry and I had no clear suspects in the murder investigation or the arson case. Sure, Dirk had showed off his fiery temper again. But I had found nothing to link him to the mayor's murder. As long as his alibi held, I couldn't tie him to the fire, either.

I tried calling the factory where he worked. No one answered. I'd have to wait till morning when someone would be in the office. I still had the phone in my hand when I noticed the folded paper on my desk. It was the e-mail message Janet gave me. I decided to switch gears.

I use my computer all the time in my business. It's amazing what you can find out about a person online. I've uncovered affairs and secret financial deals. I've even witnessed a few chat-room confessions.

It can be difficult to trace an e-mail back to the person who wrote it. But I knew I could at least find out *where* the message originated. I tried to look up the e-mail address on several different search engines. No luck. I finally came up with a phone number. When I called it, a fax machine screeched in my ear. The number didn't exist in any online directory.

As a last resort, I phoned Harry. "Hey," I said, "I need a favor. Can you check out a phone number for me? I'm trying to track down a lead on the fire, but I've hit a dead end."

"Sure, what's the number?" Harry asked.

"It's 804-555-7398," I told him.

"Hmmm," said Harry, "give me a second." I could hear Harry's labored one-finger typing while I waited. "Well, it looks like it's a business: JWE, Inc. There's no address—just a post office box in Richmond."

"Thanks, Harry," I said. "I'll let you know if I need help following up on this."

"Sure, Tony, anytime," Harry replied. "By the way, I got the phone number for that guy Dirk said he was with the night of the fire."

I wrote down the number and hung up. The day wasn't a complete loss, anyway. I did answer one question. I remembered from my earlier research that the main office of Jim Williams Enterprises was located in Richmond.

I thought I might find Jim Williams at the Beverly Restaurant bar, so I drove over there. It took a minute or two for my eyes to adjust to the dim light of the barroom. I ordered a beer while I scanned the place. Jim was sitting alone at a small table in the back corner. He chatted with a pretty waitress while she cleared off a nearby table.

"Mind if I join you?" I asked. I sat down before he could answer.

"I guess not," Jim said. "To what do I owe the pleasure?"

"I thought we could discuss business—your business," I said. I placed the e-mail printout on the table in front of him.

"It's kind of dark in here," he said. "Do you expect me to read this?"

"I expect you to tell me how long you've been threatening Bob Turner," I replied.

"Threatening?" he laughed. "You've got the wrong guy! This here is what I call 'friendly persuasion.' I was just trying to convince Turner to do the right thing."

"The right thing for who?" I asked. The waitress headed our way, but I shook my head and she disappeared.

"Look, he's an old man," Jim said. "He was going to retire anyway. I just thought I could persuade him to do it sooner rather than later. And the way things turned out, he should have heeded my warnings."

"And since he didn't, you burnt down his store?" I questioned.

"No way. That's not my style," Jim answered casually. "I'm a businessman. Besides, I didn't have to do anything. Someone else took care of the store. And now, Bob's in the hospital—barely alive, from what I hear. He should have quit sooner. Now, when the city council meets next month, I'll be ready to start construction."

Jim was a smooth talker. And his slow Southern drawl made him sound very sure of himself.

"And what about Mayor Cook?" I

asked. "Was he in the way, too?"

"I never had any trouble with him," Jim said. "Check the records. The mayor said that if the council agreed to let me develop downtown, he would support the plan."

Truth is, I had checked. Jim was right. He had no reason to kill the mayor. And now I was sure he hadn't set the fire. My list of suspects was growing shorter by the day.

I called the Turner house, hoping to catch Janet.

"Hello," she said. Her voice was shaky.

"Janet, this is Tony. How is Bob doing?"

"Oh, he's still in a coma," she said. "The doctors say his body just shut down when his heart stopped. We still don't know if he'll wake up."

"I'm sorry," I told her. "I hope everything will be OK. The reason I called is that I wanted to put your mind at ease about that e-mail you showed me. It was Jim Williams trying to scare you into selling out."

"Are you sure?" Janet asked. "How do you know he won't do something else? Maybe he's the one who shot the mayor."

"No, I don't think so," I said. "He's harmless. He won't be bothering you anymore."

Chapter 12

The first thing on my mind when I woke up was to check out Dirk's alibi. I called the factory in Fairmont. The secretary forwarded my call to the line supervisor, Mr. Wallace.

"Wallie here," he said gruffly.

"Mr. Wallace," I began, "I'm Tony Jefferson. I'm working on an arson case for the Stanton police department. I'd like to ask you a question about Dirk Turner."

"Turner?" he asked. "What do you want with him?"

"Could you tell me how late he worked on the night of February 4th?"

"Hang on while I look in the book," he grumbled. I heard pages rustling. "Yeah, here it is. We worked late that night, finishing up a big job. Turner was here till 9:45. Then we all went out for a drink."

"You were with him?" I asked.

"Yup. There must have been a dozen of us. We went to a local joint and ordered burgers and beer. We start in at 6 A.M. here, so it was a long day."

"And Dirk was with you the whole night?" I asked.

"He sure was. I remember he talked to his wife a couple of times that night. He called her to tell her where we were and that we were just going to get a quick bite. Then time got away from us. That woman actually called the bar later to check up on him! It must have been around midnight. She was pretty mad."

"Thanks," I said. "You've been a big help."

Well, I had already narrowed the arson down to two suspects. Now I was sure I knew who set the fire. And it wouldn't be fun telling Harry. This was one crime I was not enjoying solving.

Julie called and invited me to lunch. We met at a coffee shop a couple of blocks from my office. We settled into a booth and ordered bowls of chili.

"I've been thinking about the Turner Building," Julie said. "I doubt Bob Turner set the fire. If he did, then he wouldn't have run after you like that."

"You're right, Julie," I replied. "Bob didn't do it. I'll bet the reason he was so upset was because he figured out who it was."

"What do you mean?" Julie asked.

"I'm pretty sure that Janet set the fire," I told her. "She had the best motive. She knew her husband wasn't well. And they needed the insurance money to retire."

"Oh, no," said Julie. "Janet burned down her husband's business?"

"It makes perfect sense," I said. "She was worried about Bob's health. And she knew how much the insurance was worth. Bob's policy pays almost twice what Jim Williams offered them for the building. Plus, it might have given them enough to loan Dirk some money, too."

"I remember seeing a movie once where the murderer was the one person who just couldn't stop talking about it," Julie said. "Janet was like that. She tried to blame it on Nancy. And she kept coming to talk to you to distract you from suspecting her!"

"But I suspected her all along," I said. "She had motive and opportunity, and she knew she could slip in and set the fire without being noticed. She just didn't count on anyone else being in the building."

"You mean the mayor?" Julie asked.

"The mayor and the mayor's killer," I said matter-of-factly. "Janet was still in the building when the mayor was killed."

"You mean there's a witness?" Julie asked with surprise.

"Well, she may not have seen the murder," I explained. "But she heard the gunshot. And the cause of death was never made public. Harry told me in confidence that Mayor Cook was shot with a small-caliber handgun. Janet slipped last night and admitted that she knew the mayor was shot."

"Then who killed him?" Julie asked.

"I believe Myra Hastings is the murderer," I replied. "I'm not quite sure of her motive, but I know she was with the mayor that night. And if Chance's nose is right, Janet set the fire before Myra left the building. She and Janet probably just missed bumping into each other."

"Wait, Tony! I think I know why she did it!" Julie cried. "When we were at the Turners', I spoke to Miss Cook. She said that her brother told her he was going on vacation to get away from Myra. He thought she was becoming obsessed with him. She imagined that they were having a relationship. And she was jealous when he went anywhere without her. He said he wasn't going to tell her about the trip until just before he left."

"So they must have argued when the plane ticket arrived," I said. "I could tell she was holding something back."

"What will happen now?" Julie asked me.

"It's all in Harry's hands," I replied. "I told him to question Myra and to test for residue from the fire on her purse. Janet is still at the hospital, watching over Bob. Harry thinks it won't take much to get her to confess."

"Well, that's it then, Tony," Julie

said. "Two more crimes solved by you and your canine partner!"

"I guess so," I told her. "But now that you know who did it, you're not going to stop dropping by, are you?" I asked with a sly smile.

"Not a chance!" Julie laughed.